THE RAINBOW TRAIL

by

JENNIFER CURRY

Illustrated by Maureen Bradley

HAMISH HAMILTON
LONDON

This book is dedicated, with love, to Sue, because it was begun on her birthday, January 8th.

HAMISH HAMILTON CHILDREN'S BOOKS

Published by the Penguin Group
27 Wrights Lane, London W8 5TZ, England
Viking Penguin Inc, 40 West 23rd Street, New York, New York 10010, U.S.A.
Penguin Books Australia Ltd, Ringwood, Victoria, Australia
Penguin Books Canada Ltd, 2801 John Street, Markham, Ontario, Canada L3R 1B4
Penguin Books (N.Z.) Ltd, 182-190 Wairau Road, Auckland 10, New Zealand

Penguin Books Ltd, Registered Offices: Harmondsworth, Middlesex, England

First published in Great Britain 1990 by
Hamish Hamilton Children's Books

The publishers are grateful to Unwin Hyman for permission to reproduce extracts from *James and the Giant Peach* by Roald Dahl.

1 3 5 7 9 10 8 6 4 2

British Library Cataloguing in Publication Data
CIP data for this book is available from the British Library

ISBN 0-241-12802-1

Typeset by Rowland Phototypesetting, London
Printed in Great Britain at the University Press, Cambridge

Chapter 1

THE CHILDREN could tell that Mr Binns was excited. He came bouncing into the classroom and clapped his hands for silence.

"Sit down, sit down," he said. "I have some important news for you." Class 2 gazed at him. "I'm sure you're going to enjoy it."

Johnny Shanks pulled a face at his friend, Alby. "I bet it's another of his silly old projects," he whispered, and Alby grinned and waggled his ears.

"Stop talking, you two," said Mr Binns. "Just listen for a change. Now, tell me, how many of you have ever been to The Playhouse at Chilbury?"

Sue Chambers' hand shot up. "My grandad takes me every year," she said proudly. "To the pantomime. Last year it was *Cinderella*, and the coach was all glass, and there were REAL mice, and . . ."

"Good-good," Mr Binns interrupted her. Sue always had a lot to say, too

much sometimes, and he was longing to get on with *his* news.

Gradually one or two hands crept up, but not many. "I'd *like* to go," said Alby White, "but my mum says it's too far away. And it costs an arm and a leg."

"Quite!" beamed Mr Binns. "Quite-quite! And that's why the theatre is coming to us. Here. To Rydon Primary School. So we can *all* enjoy it."

The children stared. Then they all began to talk at once. They peppered Mr Binns with questions.

"Oh! When?" gasped Sue.

"Sir! Can we meet the actors?" asked Johnny. "I'd like to be an actor. Get on the telly."

The others groaned and looked at each other. Johnny was the class show-off.

"You would!" said Sue. "But, Mr Binns, what are the *real* actors going to do?" And she glanced scornfully at Johnny as if he were a little worm.

"*I'm* going to be a real actor," he retorted, and stuck out his tongue at her.

"Since when?" grinned Alby. "Yesterday you were going to be an astronaut."

Mr Binns sighed and covered his face with his hands.

The only one who didn't seem to have anything to say was Tracey Biggles. Tracey was always rather quiet. She had a pale face with a lot of freckles on her nose, and her straight mouse-coloured hair was tied back in two short plaits. She hadn't been in Class 2 for very long. Her family had moved to Rydon about four months ago, just after Christmas, and she was still a bit timid and shy.

"Tracey's a dreamer," Mr Binns used to say. "Head in the clouds half the time."

Now, while the rest of the class was still in an uproar over the news, Tracey didn't say a word. But her eyes shone.

"Why can't you all be as quiet and well-behaved as Tracey?" Mr Binns demanded. "Now, if you'll just settle down . . . Right. That's better. So, two people are coming from the theatre . . ."

"Only two!" exclaimed Johnny in disgust.

Mr Binns ignored him, the way he usually did when he was being a pest.

"Two people. An actor and an actress. And they are going to stay at school with us for a week."

"A whole week?" Sue wriggled on her chair.

"For one whole week we won't have any lessons."

"Wow!" exclaimed Johnny. "Brill!"

Mr Binns pressed on. "Instead we shall be learning from the actors. They will be teaching us all sorts of things."

"What sort of things?" asked Alby.

"Well – how to make costumes and paint scenery, do sound effects, put on stage make-up . . . that sort of thing."

"Great!" said Johnny.

"And at the end of the week," Mr Binns continued, "on the Friday night, we shall all put on a play."

Suddenly Tracey put her hand up. "Which play?" she asked shyly.

"Er . . . let me see . . ." Mr Binns glanced at the paper in his hand. "*James and the Giant Peach*. That's it."

"*James and the Giant Peach*! It's my very favourite story!" said Tracey.

"Sir! Sir!" called Johnny, jumping up and waving his hand about frantically. "Can I play James? *Please*, sir."

"No, Johnny Shanks. You can not play James. You can just sit down and be quiet," snapped Mr Binns. "Have you seen the play, Tracey?"

Tracey shook her head. "No. But I've read the book. About three hundred times. It's my favourite."

"Three hundred times!" exclaimed Mr Binns. "It's a wonder you ever found time to come to school!"

Tracey's pale face flushed. "Well, perhaps not quite three hundred!" she said, and Mr Binns laughed.

"Don't worry. I'm only teasing you. Now – any more questions?"

"Yes, sir. Please. Can I be James? Please, sir," begged Johnny.

"No, you can't be James."

"But, sir . . ."

"Mrs Granville has decided that the

top class will do the acting. They'll be leaving this school in the summer, you know, so it's their only chance."

"But, sir . . ."

"Anyway, there's more to putting on a play than acting," Mr Binns went on. "That's just a very small part of it, you know. There are all sorts of marvellous things to do . . ."

"But, SIR . . ."

Mr Binns turned and glowered at Johnny. "Do stop 'butting' me, Johnny," he shouted. "You're not a little GOAT, for heaven's sake. If you 'but' me just once more I'll . . . I'll . . ."

Class 2 laughed. But they never did discover exactly what Mr Binns would do to Johnny because just then the bell rang for the end of school and they all made a dash for the door.

Chapter 2

IT WAS ABOUT a month later, early in June, that the actors were due to visit Rydon. When the day arrived at last the children were almost wild with impatience. Since there were to be no proper lessons that week their headteacher, Mrs Granville, had let them all go out into the playground to welcome the theatre van. Some of them had brought flags to wave, others had football rattles, balloons and streamers. Sue had a bag of rose petals to throw, though her grandad said he thought they were supposed to be for weddings really. And Johnny Shanks had made a placard and fastened it on to a long stick. 'WELCOME TO THE ACTERS', it said, in big red letters. Johnny couldn't think why Mr Binns looked so cross when he saw it.

"Some teachers are *never* satisfied," he grumbled to Alby.

"Some teachers like you to get your spelling right," grinned Alby.

As the van trundled through the school gates, the children could hardly believe their eyes. It was painted all over in a dozen different colours. Shining, painted flowers twined around its windows, birds and huge butterflies flew across its sides, dozens of children's faces peered out from brightly-coloured trees and bushes, and the whole van was wrapped in a broad and beautiful rainbow.

Tracey looked at Sue, her eyes like saucers. "It makes me feel dizzy just looking at it."

"It makes me want to laugh," giggled Sue. "It's like a story book on wheels."

The passenger door was pushed open

and a tall, dark-haired young man jumped out. He looked around at all the balloons and bunting, and his blue eyes crinkled up into a smile. "Great!" he said, grinning around at the children, and putting both his thumbs up to show how delighted he was with their welcome. He spoke to Mrs Granville, then she led him across the yard to shake hands with Mr Binns. The children couldn't help smiling when they saw the two men together. Mr Binns always came to school in a boring grey suit and a shirt and tie. He was rather a small man, quiet and ordinary, and his clothes were quiet and ordinary too. The actor towered over him. He wore old denim trousers, a black leather jacket and red and white trainers. And in one ear he had a hooped gold earring.

"Hi!" he said, putting out his hand. "Geoff Turk's the name. Good to be here."

Mr Binns beamed. "We're glad to have you here," he said. "The children have been counting the days."

"Great!" grinned Geoff. "You must meet Mel." He turned towards the van. "Come on, love!" he yelled. "What's keeping you?"

Just then the driver's door opened and a young woman jumped lightly to the ground.

Sue stared. The actress was just about the prettiest person she had ever seen. She had huge brown eyes, and a grin that seemed to stretch from ear to ear. But it was her hair that was the really marvellous thing. It sprung out from her head in a halo of thick, corkscrew curls. Just like a silvery-gold dandelion clock.

She nodded towards them. "Hello!" she said. "I'm Melanie Winters. Mel for short."

"I'm called Sue Chambers," said Sue, sounding very important, "and this is my friend, Tracey Biggles. I think your hair's lovely – how do you get it to go like that?"

But Mel didn't answer her. She was too busy looking at Tracey. "Biggles, did you say?"

Tracey sighed. "I know. Everybody thinks it's a silly name. But I can't help it, can I? I was born with it."

"I don't think it's silly," said Mel. "My auntie used to be called Biggles – before she married my Uncle Jack. When I was little I thought it was a magic name. It always made me laugh."

"Your auntie!" exclaimed Sue.

"Perhaps you're related. Perhaps you're Tracey's long-lost cousin or something."

"That would be funny," Mel said.

"But not very likely. My family lives miles away from here."

"So does Tracey's!" said Sue. "She's just come to Rydon."

"Mel!" Geoff called again. "What's keeping you?"

"Sorry," said Mel. "I've got to go now. Talk to the teachers and meet the other kids. But I'll see you two later. OK?"

"OK," said Sue. Then she squeezed Tracey's arm. "I think she's lovely, don't you?" Tracey nodded. "But how do you think she makes her hair stick out like that?"

Tracey shrugged. "What I want to know is – what does the other one do?"

"Which other what?"

"The other man who got out of the van."

"I didn't see anybody else."

"You must have. He was tall and quite old. Thin. With a funny beaky nose. You must have seen him."

"Where is he now then?" asked Sue, as the two girls stared round the playground.

"I don't know," muttered Tracey. "He seems to have vanished. Perhaps he's gone inside."

"Look!" exclaimed Sue. "They're *all* going inside."

Sure enough the playground was nearly empty. Geoff and Mel were being led through the front door and all the children were trooping into school behind them.

"Come on," she yelled, grabbing Tracey's hand and pulling her along. "We don't want to miss anything, do we?"

Inside, the whole school was

assembled in the big hall. The teachers and the actors sat on the platform, and the children squatted on the floor, wherever they could find a space. Sue and Tracey were the last ones to squeeze through the door, and as soon as they had sat down Mrs Granville began to speak.

"Now," she said, "I'm not going to be a teacher this week. I'm going to leave all that to Mr Geoffrey Turk and Miss Melanie Winters. All I want to do is to say how very pleased we are that they've come to spend a week of their valuable time here with us."

She sat down, and all the children shouted and clapped and whistled until Geoff stood up, laughing and holding out his hands for silence. "Thanks," he said. "From today, for one whole week, this is not a school, it's a theatre." The children cheered again. "You'll still be learning things. Lots of things. You'll be learning exactly what happens when we put on a play. But you'll not be pupils. You'll be actors, and scene painters, and property makers, and carpenters, and wardrobe assistants, and printers. Yes, all of those – and more. And together – together – we are going to make MAGIC."

And this time the children roared and shouted so much that they nearly blew the roof off with their cheering.

Chapter 3

WHEN ALL THE children had gone back to their own classrooms, Mr Binns handed out copies of the play to Class 2. They looked through the pages and gazed at the wonderful pictures until Geoff and Mel came in to talk to them about what they were all going to do. Mr Binns left his place at the front of the room and went to the back, to sit in the special Reading Chair. The children tried not to giggle when they saw him squashing himself in behind the Reading Table, clutching his book in his hand and trying to pretend he was just an ordinary member of Class 2.

"Sir!" said Johnny, jumping up and waving his hand at Geoff. "Can I be James, sir? I'm going to be an actor when I leave school."

Mr Binns gave a cross cough from his corner and glared at Johnny. He opened his mouth to tell him to sit down and be quiet, but then he remembered he'd stopped being the teacher for a few days so he closed his mouth again and managed to keep it firmly shut.

Geoff just grinned. "I'm not 'sir'," he said. "I'm Geoff. And the answer's 'no', Johnny, because all the actors are coming from the top class."

"All except me," laughed Mel. "I'm going to be the narrator."

"I don't even know what a narrator is," grumbled Johnny. "Do you, Alby?"

Alby was the clever one in the class. Usually he knew everything. But this time he just waggled his ears, winked his left eye and shrugged his shoulders all at the same time, which Johnny thought was his cleverest thing yet.

"Does anybody know?" asked Mel. "What about you, Tracey?"

Tracey flashed her a quick, shy smile. "I think I do. Is it another name for the storyteller?"

"Well done," Mel nodded. "The thing is," she continued, "we happen to know that this class is very good at making things."

"Yeah!" exclaimed Geoff. "I saw the fairground you built. In the library at Easter."

The children looked at each other and opened their eyes wide. Their Rydon Fair project had been the most exciting thing they'd ever done but they'd never thought that people like Geoff Turk would go to see it. Not people who didn't even live in the town.

"Louise Richards, the lady in the Children's Library, is a friend of mine," Geoff explained. "She told me it was too good to miss, so I came over specially. I thought it was great."

"So," said Mel, "we reckoned you would be the right class to make the costumes, didn't we, Geoff? In this play there are all sorts of weird insects. Big ones, the size of children . . ."

"Ugh!" Sue shuddered.

"Nice, friendly insects!" Geoff grinned. "And we can show you how to make super bodies for them, out of cardboard boxes, and paint, and string and stuff."

"Insect *bodies*!" snorted Johnny.

"Bor-ING!"

"Sounds all right to me," said Alby.

"Good," Geoff said. "Anything anybody wants to know before we start work?"

Sue put up her hand. "Are there just going to be two of you helping us, or did you bring somebody else?"

"Just two of us, I'm afraid," Mel

laughed. "*We* are The Rainbow Theatre Company. 'Rainbow' for short."

Sue pulled a face at Tracey as if to say 'I told you so', and Tracey blushed scarlet.

Geoff looked at them curiously. "Why?" he asked. "Were you hoping there'd be more of us?"

"Oh no!" explained Tracey, embarrassed. "It's just that I thought I saw a man getting out of your van. He was tall and thin, with a big beaky nose."

Mel frowned. "How strange."

"I guess it was just a passer-by," suggested Geoff. "Decided to drop in and see what all the excitement was about."

"That must be it," Mel agreed. "It's the van that does it. Pulls 'em in like bees to a honeypot. But *officially* there are only the two of us."

Suddenly Geoff looked at his watch. "Look, we've got to get on and see the other classes. So – you're in charge of the insect costumes – is that agreed?"

All the children nodded except Johnny, who opened his mouth to argue again, but this time Mr Binns couldn't stop himself from taking charge.

"Yes!" he said firmly. "That IS agreed."

"Great!" said Geoff. "You read through the play with Mr Binns now. We'll be back later with the boxes and stuff to get you started. See you."

When Tracey got home from school her mum looked at her in amazement. Her cheeks were as rosy as red apples and her face bright with excitement.

"Whatever's got into you?" she

asked. "You look all . . . bubbly."

Tracey had so much to tell her about Rainbow that her words came tumbling out as she explained all the things that Geoff and Mel had been doing.

"Mel's a funny sort of name," Mrs Biggles interrupted her. "What's he like?"

"It's not a he, it's a she!" exclaimed Tracey. "And the really funny thing is, she has an auntie who was called Biggles before she married her uncle. Mel's uncle, I mean! Sue thought we might be related, but Mel said she didn't think so because her family lived a long way from here."

"Where?"

"I don't know. She didn't say . . . Mum . . ."

"Yes?"

"Do you think I could be an actress

when I'm grown up?"

Just then Tracey's dad came in from work. "Is there a cup of tea on the go?" he called through the door.

"Never mind tea. You come in here and look at this daughter of yours," Mrs Biggles said. "She's got stars in her eyes."

"Why is that then?" Tracey's dad asked.

"She thinks she might like to go on the stage, would you believe?"

Mr Biggles sat down and stared at Tracey. "Good heavens!" he exclaimed. "They always say it runs in the blood."

Tracey felt rather alarmed. When she'd told her mum that she thought she'd like to work in the Post Office, Mrs Biggles had just said, 'That's a good idea.' She certainly hadn't told dad all about it. But now they were both sitting there looking at her and saying it 'ran in the blood' as if she'd caught a nasty disease or something. "What do you mean?" she asked.

"Well, you wouldn't be the first Biggles to get stage-struck," her dad said. "There's been an actor in the family before now."

"Who?" asked Tracey. "You never told me."

"My grandfather." Her dad shook his head slowly. "He was a sad case."

"Why? What happened?"

Her mother took up the story. "*He* said he gave up acting for Emmeline, your great-grandma. He said she wanted him at home, not traipsing the country from one theatre to the next. But it wasn't really that, was it, Bri?"

"No." Mr Biggles tapped his head. "It was his memory!"

"Poor thing!" said Tracey. "You mean he couldn't remember his lines?"

"He could remember his lines perfectly. He just couldn't remember which play he was in. Once, when he was supposed to be Macbeth, out he came with Hamlet's 'To be, or not to be'."

Tracey's mum giggled, but Mr Biggles was serious. "It wasn't funny, Tracey. Just imagine if your James forgot about the Giant Peach and thought he was Charlie in the Chocolate Factory. Halfway through the play, I mean. You wouldn't think that was funny, would you?"

Tracey shook her head, but Mrs Biggles laughed and hurried off to the kitchen to put the kettle on.

"What happened to him?" Tracey asked in a worried way.

"It was a shame really. They gave him one or two odd jobs to do back stage but he was hopeless. Kept losing things, or bumping into the scenery. So, he drifted off and got himself a job as a chauffeur. He said he liked dressing up in the uniform! But whenever he got anywhere near a theatre, even when he was quite old, in he would go and wander around the stage like a ghost. 'It's the smell of the grease paint,' he used to say. 'It never lets you go.'"

"Poor thing!" said Tracey again. "Poor old man!" And tears filled her eyes for the great-grandfather she had never known.

"Come on now, cheer up," said Mrs Biggles as she brought in the tray and laid it down on the table. "Have some tea, the pair of you, and let Grandad Biggles rest in peace."

Chapter 4

BY WEDNESDAY MORNING Class 2's room had turned into a state of cheerful chaos. The pink wall at the far end, where usually the children's own pictures were fastened up, was now covered with great big drawings of a spider, a centipede, a grasshopper and a ladybird, along with diagrams which showed exactly how to make them. Mr Binns' table was piled high with pots of paint and brushes, mounds of paper fasteners, scissors and string. All the desks had been pushed back against the walls, and the floor was littered with

tracing paper, brightly-coloured squares of sticky paper and heaps of boxes and cardboard.

Sue was good at drawing so she was in the group that had been set to work tracing out the shapes of wings and legs. Johnny had appointed himself chief cutter, and he crawled over the cardboard, carefully cutting along the lines of soft black crayon. Alby and his team were 'fixers'. They had the job of fixing all the different bits together to make sure that they worked properly, and there were screams of laughter as the grasshopper waggled his wings and waved his funny, crooked legs. Tracey was one of the 'finishers', adding the final little details. The insect she liked best was the ladybird.

"Come and help me with her spots," she said to Sue. So Sue went and stood

LADYBIRD
Wings
CUT SIX
HEAD
overlap
and fix with clips
CUT SIX
pipe cleaners
antennae
SPIDER'S
BALLOON
RED

beside her, wetting the circles of black gummed paper on a sponge for Tracey to stick all over the ladybird's shiny red shell.

"Make sure you press them on really hard," warned Mel, who had come in to see how they were getting on. "It would be terrible if they started to drop off during the performance."

When they had finished, Tracey slithered underneath the cardboard shell and crawled around the classroom doing a funny little sideways dance and making the other children squeal and jump out of the way, until they all

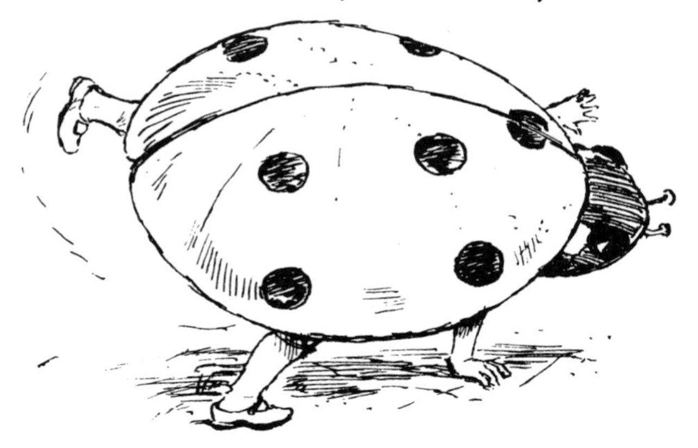

collapsed on the floor in a squirming, giggling heap.

"I was told you were a shy, *quiet* girl," Mel laughed as she extricated the ladybird from the tangle of waving arms and legs. "'Tracey wouldn't say boo to a goose', I was told. But I'm beginning to think Mr Binns must have got you all wrong."

When the bell rang for play-time none of the children wanted to go out. They were all far too busy.

"I don't believe this," declared Mr Binns. "Usually you're out through that door like a herd of stampeding elephants. Now I can't get rid of you."

Johnny made a loud trumpeting noise, put his head down, and charged around the class room. "I'm a stampeding elephant!" he yelled.

Mr Binns groaned. "Out!" he

bellowed. "Out of my sight, the lot of you. But mind you don't get blown away – there's a wind getting up out there."

As the children tumbled out of doors the summer wind buffeted them about, snatching at the girls' skirts, tugging their hair, blowing up dust in their faces.

"Ouch!" cried Tracey. "I've got some dirt in my eye."

"I can do it," said Sue, dragging her into a sheltered corner. "Stand still and open your eye as wide as you can." Then, very gently, she wiped away the speck of dirt with the corner of her hanky. "All right now?"

Tracey blinked, screwed up her eyes, blinked again, and smiled with relief. "Brilliant!" she said. "It's gone."

Sue grinned. "I'm going to be a nurse

when I leave school. Or maybe a doctor." Then she went haring off down the playground to catch up with the others.

Tracey was just about to follow her when suddenly her attention was caught by a tiny splash of red on a green leaf near her head. She looked carefully and saw that it was a ladybird, browsing on the old yellow rose that scrambled up the side of the school. "I'd better have a good look at it," she thought. "Make sure we've got the right number of spots on *our* ladybird." As she was craning her neck forward, peering intently at the black marks on the insect's back, she had the strangest feeling that someone was watching her. She gave a little shiver and looked round, but there was no one there. She turned back to the ladybird and began to count the spots, one . . . two . . . three . . . Then, again, she felt that there was somebody very close to her. She swung round and there, where a few seconds before there had been only an empty yard, was an old man. She recognised him at once. It was the same old man she had seen getting out of the Rainbow van on Monday. She stared at him. He smiled and slowly beckoned to her with a long white hand.

Tracey felt frightened. She glanced anxiously round the playground but the other children were playing a noisy game, rushing about in the wind. Even if she shouted, they would never hear her. She looked back at the old man. Still he smiled and beckoned.

"What do you want?" she asked, her voice wobbly with fear.

But the old man didn't say a word.

He just went on smiling and beckoning with his thin bony fingers.

Tracey didn't want to go to him. She knew she wasn't supposed to talk to strangers. But she couldn't stop herself. She felt like a wound-up toy. Very slowly, very stiffly, she began to walk towards him, her legs taking her away from the wall and out across the playground as if she were a walking, talking doll.

"What do you want?" she said again.

But before the words were out of her mouth she heard a loud smashing noise behind her. She twisted round and saw a line of tiles crashing off the roof and down into the playground. They hurtled down with such force that when they hit the ground they broke into a hundred pieces. Tracey's heart thumped. The tiles, blown off by the wind, had landed on the exact spot where she had been standing just a moment before, looking at the ladybird. If she hadn't moved, if the old man hadn't beckoned her . . .

She turned back to thank him. "You saved me . . ." she began, but then her face went blank. The old man was nowhere to be seen. He seemed to have melted away into the air.

"Tracey, are you all right?" Mr Binns' worried voice cut into her trance as he came puffing across the yard, followed by Alby and Sue, whose game had been interrupted by the frightening noise.

"You're white as a sheet," exclaimed Sue. "Isn't she, Alby?"

Alby nodded. "Yep."

"I think you'd better come inside, out of the wind," Mr Binns said. "You didn't get hurt, did you?"

Tracey shivered. "No, I didn't get hurt," she said, in a strange little voice. "There was . . ." But just as she began to tell him about the old man and how he'd coaxed her away from the dangerous corner, the words dried up in her mouth. If Mr Binns knew the stranger was still hanging around there'd be an awful fuss. People weren't allowed to wander about in the school yard, so if he came back again everyone would be very cross with him. But Tracey knew that he had saved her from a nasty accident. Whoever he was, wherever he had come from, he must be her friend. And somehow she knew she must try to keep him her own special secret. She decided she'd better not tell her mum and dad, just in case they worried. In fact, she'd better not tell anyone, not even *Sue*.

Chapter 5

ON THURSDAY, when Class 2 had finished making their insect bodies, Mr Binns said they could take them to the school hall.

Johnny led the way. The other children usually let him be the leader because he enjoyed it so much. At home he had three big sisters who were always teasing him and bossing him about, so at school he liked to be important whenever he had the chance. Now he took his place at the front of the weird procession. "Make way! Make way!" he called out in a loud voice, trying to sound like the ringmaster in the circus. "Here come the insects. Make way for Mr Centipede, Mr Grasshopper, Miss Spider and, your very own, Miss Ladybird."

The hall was full of children, but as Johnny and the others walked slowly

forward, carrying their precious creations, they all fell back to let them go through. And when they saw the wonderful creatures they were bringing with them, they all laughed and clapped and cheered them on their way.

Geoff came running forward to meet

them. "Great!" he smiled. "Well done! They're *terrific!*"

Then Mel jumped down from the stage and hurried across to join them. "I told you they were working miracles in Class 2, didn't I?"

Geoff nodded. "You certainly did. But . . . wow!" He shook his head in amazement. "Just wait till the audience sees this lot. They'll bring the house down."

Mel put her hand on Johnny's shoulder. "I think we'd better find a nice safe corner for them, don't you? It would be dreadful if they got damaged. Come on, we'll take them backstage."

The children trooped along behind her and at last managed to find a table where their insects could not be knocked over or trodden on.

"Thanks!" said Mel. "That's

marvellous. They'll be all right there. Now, why don't you go and have a good look around and see what the other kids have been up to?"

As Class 2 gazed about them they could hardly believe their eyes. They were no longer in their shabby old hall, with its high ceiling and tall, arched windows. The place had been transformed.

"It's been turned into a real theatre!" gasped Sue. "Just like The Playhouse, only better."

Alby nodded. "Look. It's even got a ticket office."

Just beside the front door someone had put a big old school cupboard. Its double doors were wide open, and every inch of it, both inside and out, was covered with bright, colourful posters that had been painted in the art room.

Its shelves were piled high with tickets and programmes that the publicity group had made on the school's word-processor, and there was a table in front of it, with a cash box and a seating plan. Alby noticed that there were already a lot of crosses on the plan, and each cross meant a booked seat. "It's going to be packed out!" he said.

Sue took Tracey's hand and dragged her off to explore all the other marvellous things that had changed their school hall into a fairyland. From the ceiling hung twirling mobiles of big white seagulls, vivid rainbows and fluffy cotton-wool clouds. Tinsel 'rain' streamed down in long, silvery strips, and little blobs of white and shiny grey had been painted on to the walls to look like hailstones and snowflakes. On the platform, which was now a proper stage framed on all sides with long curtains, some boys were putting the finishing touches to a cardboard house standing inside its own little picket fence, and down below, on the floor at the front of the hall, there were piles of bright green cardboard bushes and red and yellow paper flowers. Katey Simpson, a chubby little girl from Class 1, was struggling to heave a mound of strange shapes up on to the stage and Sue and Tracey raced across to help her. When they got close they could see that the shapes were cardboard waves, painted a wonderful watery greeny-blue.

Mel waved to them from the stage. She was busy examining Mrs Granville's chair, which she was going to sit in when she was the narrator. Tracey and Sue smiled up at her.

"Look," she said, "we're going to

cover the chair with this lovely soft blue material, so that it seems as if I'm floating in the sky, and *this* is what I'm going to wear." She shook out a long soft silky dress, broadly striped in rainbow colours.

"Oh!" exclaimed Sue. "I think it's beautiful."

"So do I," grinned Mel. "And when Geoff turns the spotlight on me, I'll be a real dazzler, you'll see."

"Where are the lights?" asked Tracey.

"All over the place." Mel jumped down from the stage and stood beside her. "There are lots of spotlights hanging from the beams. See? *And* a

follow-spot. That one can move around and follow the actors all over the stage."

Tracey looked puzzled. "But where will they be worked from?"

"Ah! From the switchboard. Geoff has rigged that up just behind the curtain. To the left of the stage there."

"Just beside where you're going to sit?"

Mel nodded. "Yes," she said. "Geoff has to be near me because he shares my mike. He's doing the music, you know, as well as the lights."

Just then Geoff came wandering across the stage, with Johnny tagging along behind him, carrying a reel of cable in his hands.

"I'm just going to do the wiring now," he told Mel. "Then we'll be ready for the technical rehearsal. I've told Mrs Granville we'll be having the dress rehearsal tomorrow afternoon."

"What's a dress rehearsal?" Sue asked.

"Don't be stupid!" said Johnny. "Everybody knows that. It's where all the actors try on their costumes to see if they fit properly. Isn't that right, Miss?"

"No, it's not right, Johnny. The dress rehearsal is usually the very last run-through before the performance. Everybody wears their costumes, and all the lighting changes are done, and the sound effects and music. And we try not to have any stopping and starting. It's just like a proper performance, only there's no audience."

Suddenly there was an enormous crash from the end of the room and Tracey gave a sort of startled yelp. Everybody stopped what they were doing and gazed towards the stage.

"Look!" exclaimed Mel.

All Katey Simpson's beautiful waves had fallen over and were lying on the floor in a heap. Mr Binns came thundering down from the back of the hall, still holding a hammer in one hand and a jar of nails in the other.

"What-now? What-now? What-now?" he demanded. "I bet it's that Johnny Shanks again. Where *is* Johnny?"

"Sir!" protested Johnny. "That's not fair, sir. I was helping Geoff, sir."

Alby jumped on to the stage and began lifting up the cardboard waves one by one. "It's all right," he called. "There's nothing broken."

"That's OK then," said Mel. "Perhaps Katey didn't quite manage to stand them up properly. No harm done."

Katey screwed up her fat little cheeks

as she tried not to cry. "I did t-try to do it properly . . ." she stammered.

"No!" Tracey said suddenly. She didn't want to tell them what she had just seen, but she couldn't let poor Katey take the blame. "It wasn't Katey's fault. It was that man."

"Which man?" said Mr Binns impatiently. "Whatever are you talking about?"

"The old man I saw getting out of the van on Monday. The one with the big nose."

"What nonsense!" clucked Mr Binns, but already Geoff was on the stage, peering behind the curtains, round the back of the scenery, and in all the dark corners. "There's no one here now!" he said.

"Of course there isn't!" tutted Mr Binns.

"He *was* there," insisted Tracey. "Just after the crash I looked up and saw him hurrying off through the curtains."

"Tracey!" exclaimed Mr Binns. "Either you are seeing things or you're telling stories and I don't know which is worse. It's very strange that nobody else has seen this mystery man of yours. I'm beginning to get very cross."

Geoff laid his hand on Mr Binns' arm. "It's not really such a mystery. The rest of us were too busy to notice anything. Anyway, it's probably just some lonely old chap with time on his hands. Wandered in to see what's going on."

Tracey nodded. "I think he's trying to be friendly."

"People can't just march in and out as if they owned the place," protested

Mr Binns. "What does he think this is? It's supposed to be a school!"

Then the children began to giggle because, of course, their old school hall looked nothing like a school any longer. Gradually everyone stopped worrying about the intruder and wandered back to get on with their jobs. The hall filled up again with the busy sounds of hammering, and sawing, and the low buzz of voices.

Mel grinned at Tracey. "Are you waiting for another job?"

Tracey shook her head. "Mr Binns said Sue and I could go to the library to take some posters and tickets to Mrs Richards. She's making a special display for us."

"Great! Off you go then. See you soon."

"I *like* putting on a play!" said Sue,

as she and Tracey wandered out of the school gates on their way to the library. "Much better than boring old lessons."

"Yes," sighed Tracey. "But just think – only one more day, and then it'll be all over."

Chapter 6

BY FRIDAY MORNING the children were beginning to get so excited that they could hardly manage to sit still while Mr Binns did the register. He looked at them fiercely. "This afternoon," he said, "while the dress rehearsal is going on, I want you all to busy yourselves with quiet activities." Johnny gave a loud groan. "Yes, Johnny. Quiet activities. I don't suppose you even know what that means, do you?"

"Sir!" exclaimed Johnny.

"It means," continued Mr Binns, "reading . . . drawing . . . model-making . . . things like that. But this morning you can all come along with me to the hall and we'll see if we can make ourselves useful. I'm sure there'll be quite a lot of people who will be needing a bit of last minute help."

Mr Binns was right. The minute Tracey walked through the door she bumped into Ian Bell who was playing the part of the Little Old Man.

"Tracey!" he yelled, "Come and help me. I can't remember my lines."

So Tracey held his book while he tried to stagger through the words of his spell. "One hundred . . . er . . . long, skinny . . . mm . . . lizard tongues . . ." he stammered.

"No!" she clucked. "It's one thousand, not one hundred. Slimy, not skinny. And they're *crocodile* tongues!"

"Oh!" he groaned, grabbing back his

book and glaring at it in despair. “I’ll never learn it in time.”

“Yes, you will,” said Tracey kindly. “Come on, I’ll go through it with you.”

As they went off to find a quiet corner they nearly fell over Glow-worm and Earthworm who were shimmering around the hall, trying to get used to their costumes. Mel had helped to make them from old sheets that they had cut up, and dyed, and decorated, and they looked great, except that the two girls kept tripping over themselves.

"Keep practising," called Mel. "Practice makes perfect."

Johnny, who had just begun to fancy himself as a pop star, wandered off to listen to Geoff running through the songs. He was strumming away at his guitar while, in a funny, high, creaky voice, the Centipede sang:

"A rather smelly jelly
Made of armadillo's toes."

Johnny laughed out loud and Geoff grinned. "Do that again tonight, my friend. The more laughs the better."

"Please come and help me somebody," called Benjy, the Stage Manager. "I've got to mend the axe *and* check all the props, and there's hardly any time left."

"Give me your list," said Alby. "Sue and I can do the props."

"What *are* props?" hissed Sue.

"Stage properties. They're just the things that the characters have to use while they're on stage," explained Alby. Then as he read out: "Old man – stick, paper bag . . . Aunts – money, money bag . . ." and so on, Sue trotted backwards and forwards collecting all the props together and putting them in neat little piles on a table backstage.

Before they knew where the morning had gone, the bell rang for dinner time.

"Thank you everybody," called Geoff. "All those involved in the dress rehearsal – I want you back here at one-thirty sharp. Not a minute later. The rest of you – the performance starts at seven o'clock tonight. Hope you all enjoy it."

Tracey ran across to say goodbye to Mel. "Good luck for this afternoon," she said.

Mel grinned. "Fingers crossed. Pop in at half-past three and I'll tell you how we got on."

Tracey had never heard Mel raise her voice before, but when she went back to the hall at the end of the afternoon, Mel was almost shouting. She sounded very upset. "I'm telling you, Geoff, I didn't touch the house!"

"All right, I believe you," replied Geoff. "But the fact is, the house got pushed forward a good metre and I was off stage at the time."

"And I was nowhere near it. In fact, when you think about it, there was *no one* anywhere near it when it moved."

Geoff shrugged. "Well, there must be a mighty strong draught blowing in from somewhere, that's all I can say."

Suddenly Mel saw Tracey hovering at the door, and gave her a miserable little smile. "Come on in and cheer us up," she said. "The rehearsal was a disaster." And then she told her that, though Sue and Alby had laid out the props in perfect order before lunch, they'd somehow got hopelessly mixed up and nobody had been able to find anything. As if that wasn't enough, the scenery had mysteriously moved around the stage, the lights had flickered on and off in an eerie way, and the tape recorder had made the sound of a seagull screaming when it should have been the splashing of water.

"It's almost as if we had an extra – and unwelcome – member of the company!" groaned Geoff. "I mean – what about my guitar?"

"*What* about your guitar?" asked Tracey, wide-eyed.

"It just started playing. Off stage.

All by itself. Really spooky!"

Mel gave a funny sort of shiver. "I must say I did feel a bit spooked when I heard it. But I was just being silly. Geoff reckons it must have been one of the kids. Crept in backstage from the corridor and thought he'd have a go."

Geoff stood up and stretched. "Anyway, it's no good sitting here and worrying. We've got a pile of work to get through before curtain-up."

"But is it going to be all right?" Tracey asked. "I mean, tonight's the night."

Mel pushed back her thistledown curls from her tired face. "What we always tell ourselves in the theatre," she said, "is – never mind about the rehearsal, it'll be . . ."

"All right on the night!" chimed in Geoff. And he gave Mel a bear-like hug

Tracey laughed, but she couldn't help feeling anxious. Who *was* the mysterious guitar player? She thought she knew the answer. She just hoped, if it *was* the old man, and if he *was* still wandering about backstage, he wouldn't go and do something stupid and ruin the evening performance. She couldn't bear that. They'd all worked so hard it just *had* to come out right.

Chapter 7

THAT EVENING, as the time approached for curtain-up, the school hall was humming with excitement. The big room was packed. The younger children sat on the floor at the front, the older ones behind them on small chairs and low benches, and the teachers were at the end of the rows to make sure they behaved themselves. From the middle of the hall, stretching right to the back, sat all the mums and dads, friends and relations. At last the school clock began to chime seven. The murmur of conversation died away and the lights went down just as the curtains opened and the stage lights brightened. There were gasps when the audience saw the pretty white house set in its garden of bright flowers and bushes. Then a spotlight picked out Mel, smiling at them from the sky-blue chair, with her rainbow dress swirling around her. All the audience clapped and cheered, and some of the big boys whistled and stamped their feet.

Slowly Mel raised her hands and began to tell the story and, as her clear voice filled the hall, not another sound could be heard. It was as if she had cast a spell on the people listening to her. Soon they were into Scene 2 and it was time for the insects to make their first appearance. When the grown-ups saw the splendid creatures that Class 2 had made they all began to clap *again*, and

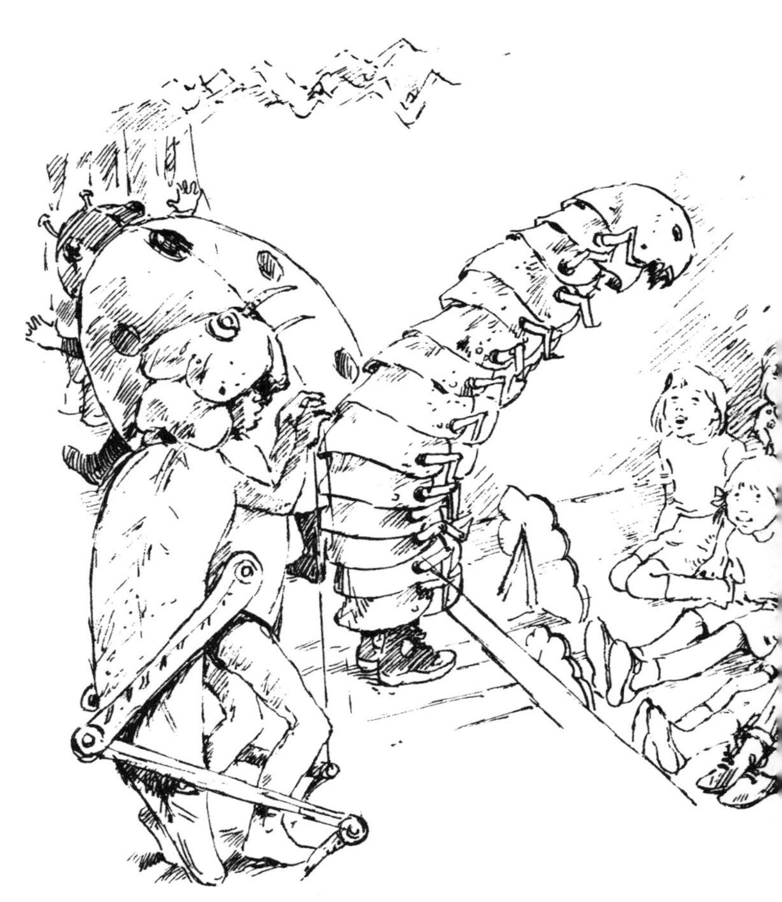

Johnny got up and turned round to give them a sweeping bow, until he noticed Mr Binns glaring at him and shaking his finger!

"I wish you'd behave yourself!" muttered Alby. "We're coming to my favourite bit – where all the insects get the giggles. They'll love this!"

Sure enough, the audience roared with laughter when they saw the strange creatures shaking and rocking from side to side as they giggled their way around the stage. Tracey watched the ladybird anxiously, and gave a sigh of relief when she saw that none of her spots had come unstuck. But then she noticed something that made her freeze in her seat. Standing in the middle of the stage, right behind James, was the thin old man. He was watching the play with delight, laughing at the insects, listening to every word with careful attention.

"What does he think he's doing?" she whispered, half out loud. But even as

she spoke the man turned and walked, very slowly, off stage, seeming to pass within an inch of Mel's chair. Mel gave a little shiver, and blinked, but then she just went on gazing out in front of her as if . . . as if he just wasn't there.

Tracey could hardly believe her eyes. She jumped to her feet.

"Where are you going?" hissed Sue. "Sit *down!*"

But Tracey was already on her way, wriggling along the row and slipping silently down the aisle. She was concentrating so hard that she didn't realise that Mr Binns was watching her. A minute later Tracey had found her way backstage, to the very spot where the thin man should have been. She looked all round her carefully but he wasn't there. She threw open the door that led out into the corridor. He was nowhere to be seen. She peered behind the curtain that hung at the back of the stage. The dark space was quite empty. Defeated, she went back to the down-stage exit where she had begun her search. Usually Geoff was there, working the lights and tape recorder, but now he was on stage for the Centipede's first song. Tracey had just made up her mind that it was safe for her to slither back into the hall when suddenly she realised that there was something wrong. She could smell a strange, sharp smell. Anxiously, she turned her head. She could smell . . . burning. At first she couldn't think where it was coming from but then her eyes fell on Geoff's switchboard, and she gasped with fear. From the top of it crept a tiny, curling wisp of smoke, and the smell was getting stronger and stronger. She looked about her frantically, wondering what to do. The switchboard was very near the stage curtain. If it burst into flames the curtain would catch fire immediately. And just beyond the curtain sat Mel, all unsuspecting, her rainbow dress spread around her feet.

Tracey opened her mouth to scream "FIRE", but suddenly she saw Mr Binns edging his way into the lighting corner, wrinkling his nose up at the stench and gazing in alarm at the thickening smoke. He nodded at Tracey and put his finger to his lips.

"Don't shout," he whispered. "You'll just make the audience panic. We must deal with this ourselves. There's a fire extinguisher over there . . ."

"Whatever is going on?"

The sound of Geoff's voice stunned Tracey. In her confusion she hadn't realised that the song had finished and he had made his exit. Unable to speak, she lifted her hand and pointed to the switchboard. With one bound Geoff was beside it, clicking off switches, disconnecting the damaged wires. There was a little murmur of surprise from the audience as the stage was plunged into darkness but almost at once Geoff was able to turn on the houselights so that no one had time to feel scared. He stared at Tracey and Mr Binns, still totally baffled by the sight of them together in his corner.

"Thanks," he said. "I don't know what you're doing here, but somehow you've saved us all from something really nasty. Now, I must get out there . . ."

He hurried back on to the shadowy stage, arriving just as the Centipede was saying his first line from Scene 4 – "Let's have some light" – and the audience howled with laughter. Geoff grinned sheepishly.

"I'm afraid we've had a slight

technical hitch," he said. "I suggest we take our interval now. But, come back here in twenty minutes and I promise we will positively DAZZLE you with the second half of – *James and the Giant Peach*!"

Everyone trooped out of the hall. Tracey followed them but no sooner had she got out of the door than she felt Mr Binns' hand on her shoulder.

"Not so fast, young lady," he said. "I think you and I had better have a chat. We'll go into the classroom – we won't be disturbed in there."

When they reached Class 2 he sat down at his table and made Tracey pull up a chair close beside him. "Now," he said, "it was very clever of you to discover the fire. Well done. Geoff says some of the wiring had rotted. Nobody's fault – it was just old and worn out. But if you hadn't noticed it right at the beginning – well, who knows what might have happened." Tracey smiled shyly, but Mr Binns hadn't finished. "What I want to know though is – what were you doing backstage in the first place? You should have been in your seat."

Tracey gulped. "The old man. I saw him walk across the stage. I just wanted to find him. Tell him he mustn't spoil our play."

Mr Binns stared and shook his head. "Not that old man of yours again!" Tracey nodded. "Well," Mr Binns continued, "this is getting beyond a joke. You'd better go back to the beginning and tell me everything you remember about him."

Tracey took a deep breath, then poured out the whole story of how she had seen him first in the playground on Monday, then hurrying off stage on Thursday, and finally, strolling across the stage during that night's performance. But she didn't say anything about the way he had saved her from the falling tiles. Somehow she wanted that to be her own special secret.

"Three times," said Mr Binns. "Yet no one else has seen him at all."

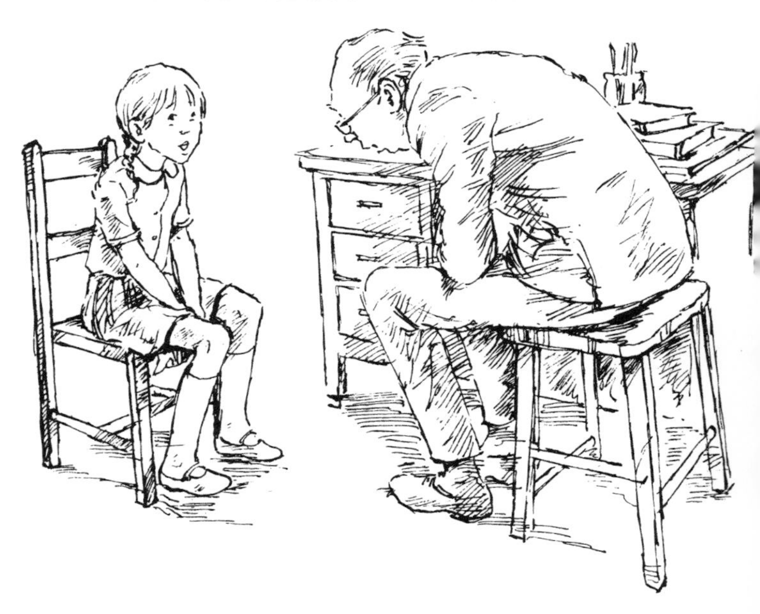

"I've been wondering about that," said Tracey. "But, with the play and everything, there's always so much happening, so many things to look at . . . I mean, tonight when I saw him, the stage was full of people, James, and Mel, and the insects. It's just that I happened to be looking where he was . . ." Her voice trailed away.

"Tracey," Mr Binns said sternly, "you're not making it all up, are you?"

Tracey flushed. "No! Nobody believes me but I *know* he's there."

"Very well then. Now, what does he look like? Exactly?"

"Tracey racked her brains but all that she could remember was that he was quite tall, rather old, with tidy brushed-down, dark hair, and a big beaky nose.

"It's not much to go on," complained

Mr Binns. "What was he wearing?"

Tracey screwed up her face. "Nothing very special. Just a sort of suit. A bit old-fashioned. Grey, I think . . . I didn't notice." Mr Binns took out his handkerchief and mopped his brow, and suddenly Tracey's eyes lit up. "He had a hanky."

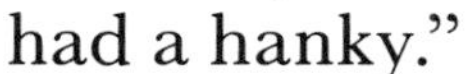

"A hanky?" Mr Binns stared at her.

"Yes. A big blue and white spotted hanky, flopping out of his top pocket. I did notice that. Dark blue with big white spots on it. I remember now. It reminded me of putting the spots on the ladybird."

Mr Binns shrugged and looked at his watch. "I think it's time we got back to our seats now. But I might just ask your mother to bring you along to the school tomorrow to have a chat with PC Matthews. He's probably quite harmless, this old chap, but I don't think we can have him wandering about all over the school. Really I don't."

Tracey shook her head sadly, and trailed back into the hall. Somehow she felt like a traitor.

Chapter 8

THE SECOND HALF of the play sped by like a dream. The audience was enchanted as the giant peach finally came to rest on top of the Empire State Building. When the actors lined up to take their bow everybody stood up and cheered themselves hoarse, and as the people wandered off home their faces were shining with pleasure.

Afterwards, all the children who had helped with the play had been invited to stay behind with their parents, to have a party in the hall, and to say goodbye to Rainbow. Tracey could hardly wait to introduce her mum to Mel, who was laughing and chatting to Mr Binns.

"Hello!" said Mrs Biggles, as they shook hands. "I'm Peggy Biggles. Tracey tells me you've got a Biggles in your family too."

"Yes!" Mel nodded. "My Auntie Ivy. She's married to my father's brother Jack."

"That's amazing!" said Tracey's mum. "Brian – my husband – has cousins called Ivy and Jack. But their name is Watson, not Winters."

"*My* name is Watson!" cried Mel. "Winters is just my stage name."

"The Watson's of Frensham, you mean? Well, that's THEM. What an amazing coincidence!"

Sue jumped up and down with excitement. "You lucky thing, Tracey.

You see, I told you, didn't I? You and Mel *are* long-lost cousins. I *knew*."

"Wow!" Mel grinned at Tracey. "What a turn-up! We must do something to mark the occasion." She closed her eyes to think, then gave a shout of triumph. "I know! You must have my Rainbow brooch."

"I couldn't!" breathed Tracey.

"I insist!" laughed Mel. She unfastened the little painted wooden rainbow she always wore and quickly pinned it on to Tracey's dress. "There!" she said. "Now you're an honorary member of The Rainbow Theatre Company."

"You lucky thing!" repeated Sue. And for the first time she wished *her* name were Biggles too.

Mrs Biggles called her husband to come over and meet Mel, then began rummaging in her handbag. "We were just telling Tracey the other day," she said, "that Bri's grandfather was an actor. Robert Biggles. Have you heard of him?" Mel shook her head. "I have a snap of him somewhere. Yes, here it is."

She pulled an old yellowing photograph from an envelope.

Mel laughed. "What a dandy! You'd never catch Geoff all spruced up like that."

"May I see?" Smiling, Mr Binns took the photograph from Mel. Then his face changed. "Have you seen this, Tracey?" he asked in a strange voice.

Mrs Biggles shook her head. "I've been looking for it all week but I didn't track it down till just after tea. I haven't had a chance to show it to her yet."

Without a word, Mr Binns handed the picture to Tracey. Tracey stared at it as if she couldn't believe her eyes.

"It's him!" she exclaimed. "Look. Look at his beaky nose."

"*And* his spotted hanky," added Mr Binns.

'Grandad always wore that," said Mr

Biggles. "It was his sort of . . . trade mark, wasn't it, Peg?"

"Yes. And always blue and white. But I still don't understand what on earth you're talking about, Tracey?" said Mrs Biggles.

"Mum! It's the old man. The one who keeps coming to school. The one on the stage."

"Don't be silly!" Tracey's mum gave an embarrassed laugh. "How could it be? It's old Grandad Biggles. And he's been dead for 20 years. What a thing to say, Tracey."

"I tell you, it's HIM. He's been here.

Watching our play."

"You do talk a lot of nonsense," said Mr Biggles. "That head of yours is full of stories . . ."

"Fairy tales and dreams!" added Mrs Biggles. "And talking about dreams . . . it's getting late. Time to go home."

"Yes," said Mel. "For all of us I think. It's been quite a day."

Gradually all the grown-ups and children straggled out of the school hall and into the playground. Mr Binns shut the doors and locked them behind him. Mel walked to the gates with Mr and Mrs Biggles and Tracey.

"'Bye," she said. "Just wait till I tell my mum and dad about meeting you – they'll be thrilled."

"Thank you for the play," said Tracey. "And thank you especially for my rainbow brooch." She put up her hand to feel it, then yelled, "I've lost it. I've dropped it. It's gone." And she burst into tears.

"Hey! Don't upset yourself," said Mel. "It's OK. I mustn't have fastened it properly. It'll be on the floor in the hall, I bet."

She ran across to Mr Binns who was just climbing into his car. "Please Mr Binns," she said, "please unlock the door so Tracey and I can go back into the hall. We've lost something."

"Something important!" sobbed Tracey.

"Oh dear!" said Mr Binns. "Oh dear! Oh dear!" But he climbed out of his car again and led the way back across the yard.

Inside the school most of the rooms and corridors were still quite light but the hall was absolutely dark, just like a real theatre. As they stepped inside, Tracey shivered.

"Doesn't it feel weird," said Mel. "So . . . cold."

"It won't take a minute," said Mr Binns, groping for the switch. But before he could find it a spotlight clicked on and shone a beam of clear white light on to the centre of the stage.

"Who did that?" demanded Mr Binns in a voice ragged with fear.

"I don't know!" hissed Mel. "Not Geoff, that's for sure. He's outside in the van."

Tracey stared at the light as if she was transfixed. She felt almost . . . hypnotised, unable to speak or move. She shivered again, and felt the little hairs prickle up on the back of her neck. Then she saw it – the outline of a man's body, gradually taking shape within the cold finger of bright light. "It's him!" she whispered. "He's here."

"I can't see anything," croaked Mel. "Oh, I can! I can!" she exclaimed.

"Whatever are you two talking about?" Mr Binns asked nervously. "There's nothing there. Nothing whatever. An empty stage, that's all." Then he gasped. "It's . . . it's the old man!"

"You can really see him?" asked Tracey.

"Yes. I . . . I can!"

"We must have brought him here somehow," said Mel. "He must have come to see our play."

Mr Binns tried to laugh. "He . . . he's been keeping an eye on his family," he stammered.

"But what do you think he wants *now*?" asked Tracey. "The play's over."

For a few moments the lonely shape of the man went on standing quietly in the centre of the light. Then, as if they were walking in their sleep, Mel and Tracey felt themselves being drawn forward up on to the stage to join him. He stood between them, calmly gazing around. Then he made a low bow.

Suddenly Mr Binns was jolted into action. "Bravo!" he called. "Well done." And he began to clap.

Somewhere in the middle of the empty hall another pair of hands, invisible hands, joined in the clapping. Then another. And another. Until at last the sound of hundreds of unseen clapping hands filled the hall and made the rafters ring with ghostly applause for Robert Biggles, the gentle old actor who had simply wanted to take his final bow. Then, inch by inch, slowly and silently, he began to disappear. He vanished away before their eyes like a flake of snow melting in a shaft of winter sunshine. And without help of human hand, the spotlight switched itself off, and the clapping stopped.

Mel, and Tracey, and Mr Binns found themselves quite alone in the dark, deserted hall. For a moment none of them spoke or stirred. It was as if they were just waking up from a strange and secret dream. Then Mr Binns cleared his throat and gave himself a little shake.

"Well," he said. "Well, well! We can't stand around like this all night, can we? Let me just switch on the lights and we'll look for that dratted brooch."

"But, Mr Binns . . ." began Tracey.

"No, Tracey. I really don't want to talk about it."

"But, Mr Binns . . ." said Mel.

Mr Binns shook his head. "Please. Something very . . . odd . . . happened here tonight. I know that. But let's just leave it there, shall we?"

He flooded the hall with light and Mel and Tracey rushed across to the place where they'd been standing earlier when Mel had made Tracey an honorary member of Rainbow. Tracey spotted the brooch almost at once.

"It's here!" she called. She pounced on it and looked at it carefully. "And it's OK. Nobody's trampled on it."

"Thank goodness for that." Mr Binns gave a sigh of relief. "Now, let's get going. The others will be wondering what on earth we've been up to." He looked at Mel and Tracey. "But we're not going to tell them, are we? It'll be our secret – just the three of us." As they hurried back along the corridor he smiled down at Tracey. "So, we won't need to talk to the police after all," he said. "There's no need to worry about our mysterious visitor any more, is there?"

"I don't think so," said Tracey.

"A nice man, your great-grandfather," Mr Binns added. "Yes, a very nice man. I'm glad we met him."

"So am I!" grinned Tracey. "And it was all thanks to Rainbow – and our play – and Mel." Then she giggled. "That first day, Geoff said we were going to make magic – and we really have, haven't we!"